H. A. REY

Curious George

rides a bike

SCHOLASTIC INC.
New York Toronto London Auckland Sydney

There are more books about Curious George. You may want to read:

CURIOUS GEORGE
CURIOUS GEORGE GETS A MEDAL
CURIOUS GEORGE TAKES A JOB
CURIOUS GEORGE FLIES A KITE

ISBN 0-590-02045-5

36 35 34 33 32   0 1 2 3 4/9

Printed in the U.S.A.   08

This is George.

He lived with his friend, the man with the yellow hat. He was a good little monkey, but he was always curious.

This morning George was curious the moment he woke up, because he knew it was a special day....

At breakfast George's friend said: "Today we are going to celebrate, because just three years ago this day I brought you home with me from the jungle. So tonight I'll take you to the animal show. But first I have a surprise for you."

4

He took George out to the yard, where a big box
was standing. George was very curious.

Out of the box came a bicycle. George was delighted; that's what he had always wanted. He knew how to ride a bicycle, but he had never had one of his own.

"I must go now," said the man, "but I'll be back
in time for the show. Be careful with your new bike,
and keep close to the house while I am gone!"

George could ride very well. He could even do
all sorts of tricks. (Monkeys are good at that.)

For instance, he could ride this way,
with both hands off the handle bar,

and he could ride this way,
like a cowboy on a wild bronco,

and he could also ride backwards.
But after a while George got tired of doing tricks and

went out into the street. The newsboy was just passing by with his bag full of papers. "That's a fine bike you got there," he said to George. "How would you like to help me deliver the papers?"

He handed George the bag and told him to do
one side of the street first,
and then turn back and
do the other side.

George was very
proud as he rode off
with his bag.

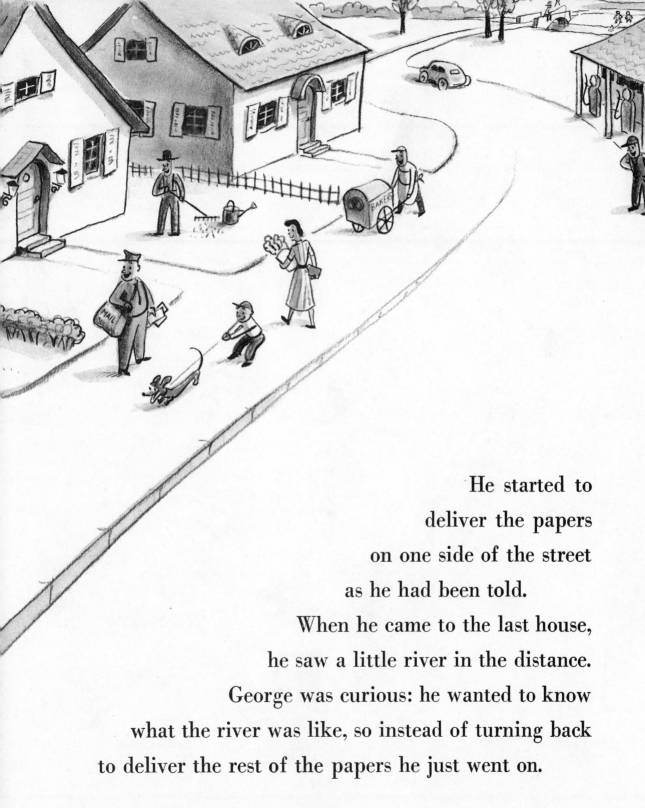

He started to
deliver the papers
on one side of the street
as he had been told.
When he came to the last house,
he saw a little river in the distance.
George was curious: he wanted to know
what the river was like, so instead of turning back
to deliver the rest of the papers he just went on.

There was a lot to see at the river:
a man was fishing from the bridge,
a duck family was paddling downstream,
and two boys were playing with their boats.
George would have liked to stop and look at the boats,
but he was afraid the boy might find out that he had
not delivered all the papers. So he rode on.

While riding along, George kept thinking of boats all the time. It would be such fun to have a boat —but how could he get one? He thought and thought —and then he had an idea.

He got off the bicycle, took a newspaper out of
the bag, and began to fold it.

First he folded down the corners, like this,

then he folded
both edges up,

brought the
ends together,

and flattened
it sidewise.

Then he turned
one corner up,

then the
other one,

again brought
the ends together

and flattened
it sidewise.

Then, gently, he pulled
the ends open —

and there was his BOAT!

Now the moment had come to launch the boat.
Would it float? It did!

So George decided to make some more boats.
Finally he had used up all the papers, and had made
so many boats that he could not count them—a whole
fleet.

Watching his fleet
sailing down the river,
George felt like an admiral.
But watching his fleet he forgot to watch where he
was going—

suddenly there was a terrible jolt: the bicycle had hit
a rock and George flew off the seat, head first.

Luckily George was not hurt, but the front wheel of the bicycle was all out of shape and the tire was blown out.

George tried to ride the bicycle, but of course it wouldn't go.

So he started carrying it, but it soon got too heavy.

Geroge did not know WHAT to do: his new bike

was spoiled, the newspapers were gone. He wished he had listened to his friend and kept close to the house. Now he just stood there and cried....

Suddenly his face brightened. Why—he had forgotten that he could ride on one wheel! He tried it, and it worked.

He had hardly started out again when he saw

something he had never seen before: rolling toward
him came an enormous tractor with huge trailers

behind it. Looking out of the trailers were all sorts
of animals. To George it looked like a zoo on wheels.

The tractor stopped and two men jumped out. "Well, well," said one of the men, "a little monkey who can ride a bike bronco-fashion! We can use you in our animal show tonight. I am the director of the show, and this is Bob.

He can straighten your wheel and fix that flat in no time, and then we'll take you along to the place where the show is going to be."

So the three of them got into the cab and drove off. "Maybe you could play a fanfare while you ride your bike in the show," the director said. "I have a bugle for you right here, and later on you'll get a coat and cap just like Bob's."

On the show grounds, everybody was busy getting things ready for the show. "I must do some work now," said the director. "Meanwhile you may have a look around and get acquainted with all the animals.

But you must not feed them — especially the ostrich, because he will eat anything and might get very sick afterwards."

George was curious: would the ostrich really
eat anything? He wouldn't eat a bugle — or would he?
George went a little closer to the cage — and before he

knew it the ostrich had snatched the bugle and tried to swallow it. But a bugle is hard to swallow, even for an ostrich; it got stuck in his throat. Funny sounds came out of the bugle as the ostrich was struggling with it, all blue in the face.

George was frightened.

Fortunately the men had heard the noise. They came rushing to the cage and got the bugle out of the ostrich's throat just in time.

The director was very angry with George. "We cannot use little monkeys who don't do as they are told," he said. "Of course you cannot take part in the show now. We will have to send you home."

George had to sit on a bench all by himself, and nobody even looked at him. He was terribly sorry for what he had done, but now it was too late. He had spoiled everything.

Meanwhile the ostrich, always hungry, had got hold of a string dangling near his cage. This happened to be the string which held the door to the cage of the baby bear. As the ostrich nibbled at it, the door opened — and the baby bear got out.

He ran away as fast as
he could and made straight
for a high tree near the camp.

Nobody had seen it but
George — and George was not
supposed to leave his bench.
But this was an emergency,
so he jumped up, grabbed the bugle, and blew as loud
as he could. Then he
rushed to his
bicycle.
The men had
heard the alarm
and thought at first
that George had
been naughty again.
But when they saw
the empty cage and
the ostrich nibbling
at the string, they knew
what had happened.

George raced toward the tree,
far ahead of the men.
By now the bear had climbed
quite high — and this was dangerous,
because little bears can
climb up a tree easily,
but coming down
is much harder;

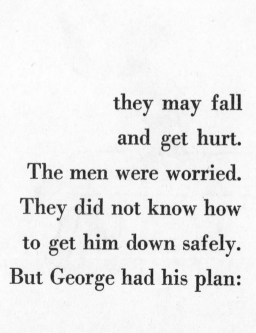

they may fall
and get hurt.
The men were worried.
They did not know how
to get him down safely.
But George had his plan:

with the bag over his shoulder, he went up the tree as
fast as only a monkey can, and when he reached the

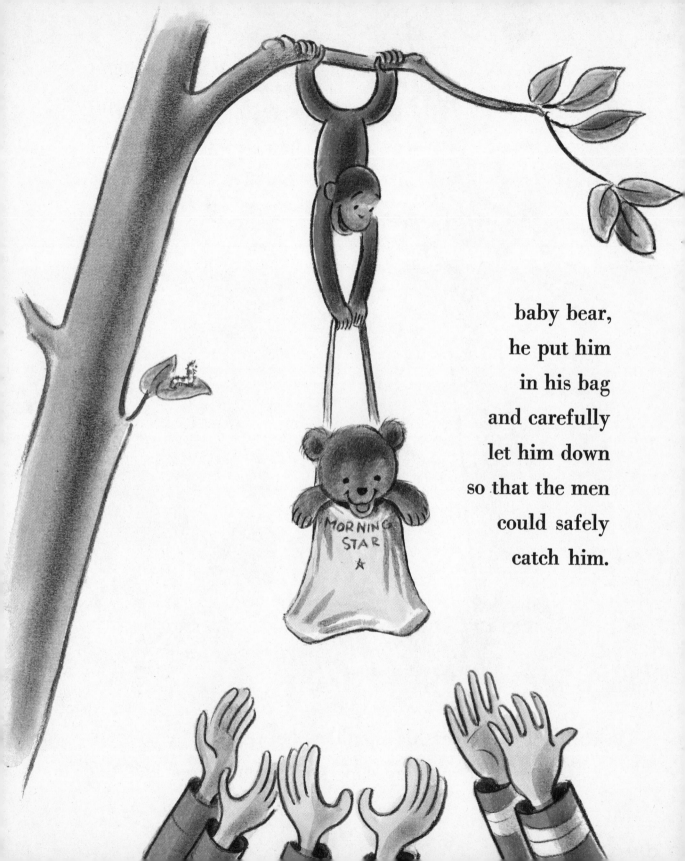

baby bear,
he put him
in his bag
and carefully
let him down
so that the men
could safely
catch him.

Everybody cheered when George had come down from the tree. "You are a brave little monkey," said the director. "You saved the baby bear's life. Now you'll get your coat back, and of course you may ride your bike and play the bugle in the show."

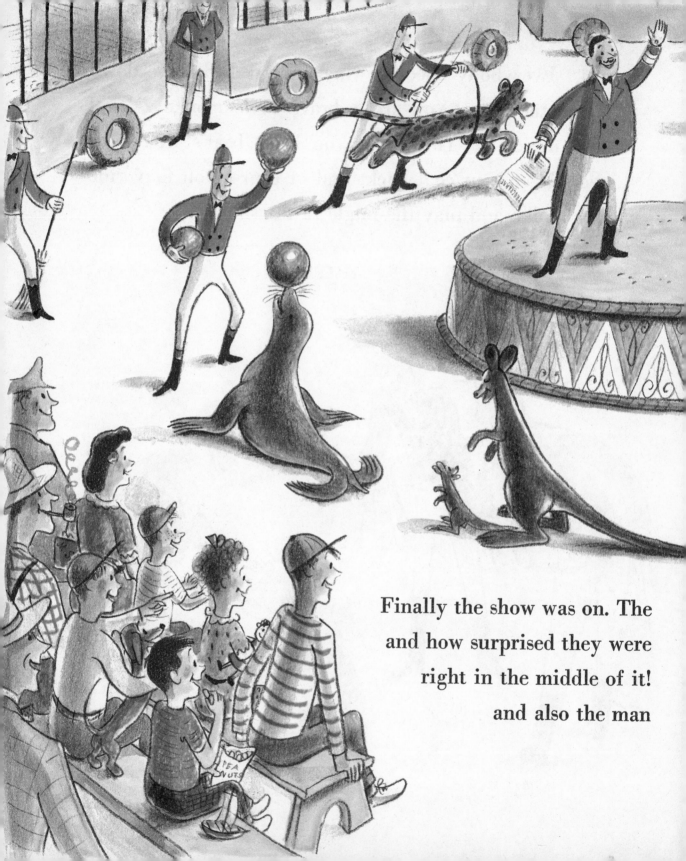

Finally the show was on. The
and how surprised they were
right in the middle of it!
and also the man

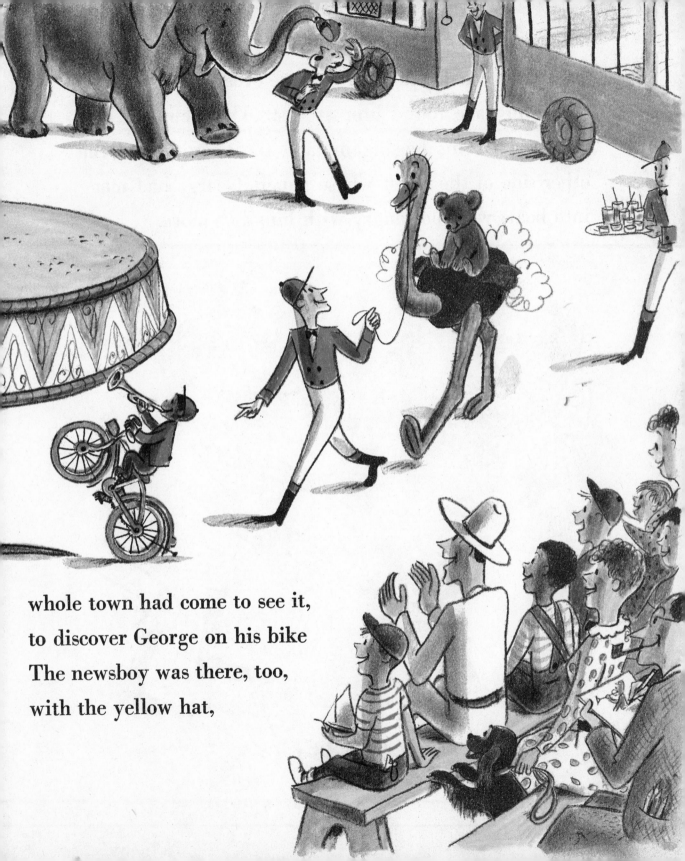

whole town had come to see it,
to discover George on his bike
The newsboy was there, too,
with the yellow hat,

who had been looking for George everywhere and was happy to have found him at last. The newsboy was glad to have his bag again, and the people from the other side of the street whose papers George had made into boats were not angry with him any more.

George!

When the time had come for George to say
good-by, the director let him keep the coat and the
cap and the bugle. And then George and his friend
got into the car and went...

good Night !